CATS

RAGDOLL CATS

by Elizabeth Andrews

Cody Koala
An Imprint of Pop!
popbooksonline.com

Hello! My name is Cody Koala

This book is filled with videos, puzzles, games, and more! Scan the QR codes* while you read, or visit the website below to make this book pop.

popbooksonline.com/ragdoll

*Scanning QR codes requires a web-enabled smart device with a QR code reader app and a camera.

abdobooks.com
Published by Pop!, a division of ABDO, PO Box 398166, Minneapolis, Minnesota 55439.

Printed in the United States of America, North Mankato, Minnesota.
102022
012023
THIS BOOK CONTAINS RECYCLED MATERIALS

Cover Photo: Getty Images
Interior Photos: Shutterstock Images; Getty Images
Editor: Grace Hansen
Series Designer: Colleen McLaren

Library of Congress Control Number: 2022941109

Publisher's Cataloging-in-Publication Data
Names: Andrews, Elizabeth, author.
Title: Ragdoll cats / by Elizabeth Andrews
Description: Minneapolis, Minnesota : Pop!, 2023 | Series: Cats | Includes online resources and index.
Identifiers: ISBN 9781098243135 (lib. bdg.) | ISBN 9781098243838 (ebook)
Subjects: LCSH: Ragdoll cat--Juvenile literature. | Cat, Domestic--Juvenile literature. | Longhair cat--Juvenile literature. | Zoology--Juvenile literature.
Classification: DDC 636.83--dc23

Table of Contents

Chapter 1
Cute as a Doll 4

Chapter 2
What's In a Name? 8

Chapter 3
Cat Care. 14

Chapter 4
Kittens 18

Making Connections 22
Glossary 23
Index. .24
Online Resources 24

Chapter 1

Cute as a Doll

The adorable ragdoll cat was created on purpose. Ann Baker fell in love with a **stray**, white, longhaired cat she named Josephine. Josephine and her kittens began the ragdoll **breed**!

Watch a video here!

bicolor

color-pointed

mitted

Ragdoll cats are large and strong. They have long fur and bushy tails. They can have a **color-point**, **bicolor**, or **mitted** coat pattern. Each type is beautiful.

Ragdolls have blue eyes.

Chapter 2

What's In a Name?

Ragdoll cats earned their name for a reason. They are known to go limp when they are picked up, just as a **rag doll** would!

Learn more here!

Ragdoll cats are happy with one person or an entire family. They are sweet and friendly. They are also quiet and calm. Ragdoll cats don't jump much, unless it is into their owner's lap for a snuggle!

Ragdoll cats should always be kept indoors. They are too sweet to fight back if they get into trouble.

Some owners say having a ragdoll cat is kind of like having a dog. Ragdolls can be taught to play fetch and come when called. They are known for turning anything into a toy!

Chapter 3

Cat Care

A ragdoll's famous fluffy coat sheds a lot. The cat should be brushed with a steel comb a few times a week. Its claws should also be clipped every two weeks.

Explore links here!

All cats need to be fed daily and have access to clean water. Their **litter box** should be cleaned daily. Cat owners should keep up with regular vet visits and get yearly shots.

Chapter 4

Kittens

Ragdoll cats usually give birth to four kittens at a time. Kittens are born deaf and blind. They will hear and see between seven and ten days old.

Complete an activity here!

Ragdoll cats might not reach their full size until they are four years old.

Ragdoll kittens are born almost all white. Their coat color and markings come with age. Kittens should be held and brushed often so they're ready for grooming when they grow up.

Making Connections

Text-to-Self

If you were to get a ragdoll cat, what kind of coat would you want it to have?

Text-to-Text

Have you read any other books about a cat with a fluffy coat? How was it similar to or different from a ragdoll cat?

Text-to-World

Ragdoll cats are too nice to fight if they're put into a dangerous situation. What are some ways an owner could protect their cat?

Glossary

bicolor – having white fur combined with fur of another color.

breed – a particular type or kind of animal.

color-point – having markings on the face, ears, nose, legs, and tail while the rest of the body is lighter.

litter box – a box filled with cat litter, which is like sand. Cats use litter boxes to bury their waste.

mitted – having front and back paws of a different color from the rest of the coat.

rag doll – a soft doll made from pieces of cloth.

stray – a domestic animal that is lost or without a home or owner.

Index

Baker, Ann, 4

body, 7–8

care, 14, 17, 21

coat, 6–7, 14

eyes, 7

kittens, 18, 21

personality, 10, 13

play, 13

rag doll (toy), 8

Online Resources

popbooksonline.com

Thanks for reading this Cody Koala book!

This book is filled with videos, puzzles, games, and more! Scan the QR codes* while you read, or visit the website below to make this book pop.

popbooksonline.com/ragdoll

*Scanning QR codes requires a web-enabled smart device with a QR code reader app and a camera.